Dear Parent:

Psst . . . you're looking at the Super Secret Weapon of Reading. It's called comics.

STEP INTO READING® COMIC READERS are a perfect step in learning to read. They provide visual cues to the meaning of words and helpfully break out short pieces of dialogue into speech balloons.

Here are some terms commonly associated with comics:
- PANEL: A section of a comic with a box drawn around it.
- CAPTION: Narration that helps set the scene.
- SPEECH BALLOON: A bubble containing dialogue.
- GUTTER: The space between panels.

Tips for reading comics with your child:

- Have your child read the speech balloons while you read the captions.
- Ask your child: What is a character feeling? How can you tell?
- Have your child draw a comic showing what happens after the book is finished.

STEP INTO READING® COMIC READERS are designed to engage and to provide an empowering reading experience. They are also fun. The best-kept secret of comics is that they create lifelong readers. **And that will make you the real hero of the story!**

Jennifer L. Holm and Matthew Holm
Co-creators of the Babymouse and Squish series

Jurassic World Franchise © 2020 Universal City Studios LLC and Amblin Entertainment, Inc. Series © 2020 DreamWorks Animation LLC. All Rights Reserved.

All Rights Reserved. Published in the United States by Random House Children's Books, a division of Penguin Random House LLC, 1745 Broadway, New York, NY 10019, and in Canada by Penguin Random House Canada Limited, Toronto. Step into Reading, Random House, and the Random House colophon are registered trademarks of Penguin Random House LLC.

Visit us on the Web!
StepIntoReading.com
rhcbooks.com

Educators and librarians, for a variety of teaching tools, visit us at RHTeachersLibrarians.com

ISBN 978-0-593-30335-1 (trade)—ISBN 978-0-593-30336-8 (lib. bdg.)—
ISBN 978-0-593-30337-5 (ebook)

Printed in the United States of America   10 9 8 7 6 5 4 3 2 1

JURASSIC WORLD

CAMP CRETACEOUS

WELCOME TO CAMP!

adapted by Steve Behling

illustrated by Patrick Spaziante

Random House 🏠 New York

The Jurassic World video game
is full of dinosaurs!
The first player to beat the game
wins a very special prize.

Camp Cretaceous is a camp
for kids at Jurassic World.
Darius can't believe it.
He's going to an island
with real live dinosaurs!

Darius is super excited!
First, he meets his camp counselors,
Roxie and Dave.
Then he meets his fellow campers.

There's Brooklynn, Sammy,
Yasmina, and Ben.
Kenji arrives by helicopter.
He acts like he owns the place.

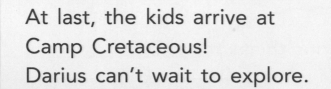

At last, the kids arrive at
Camp Cretaceous!
Darius can't wait to explore.

The kids stay in a really nice tree house.
Darius thinks it's cool!
Kenji doesn't.

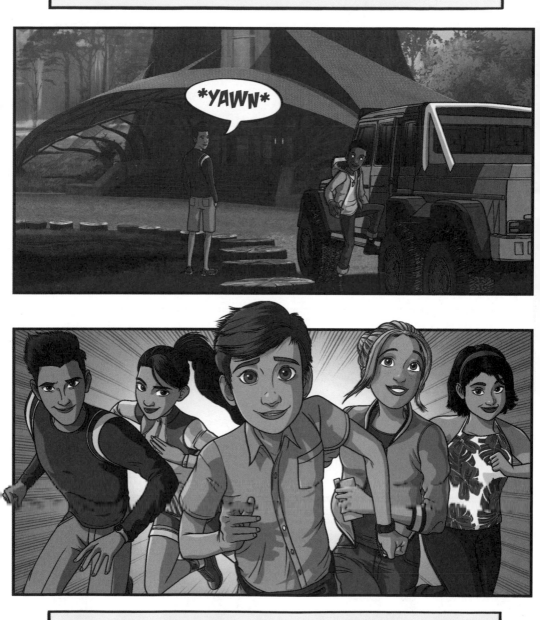

The kids race for the elevator.
They each want to get the best room . . .

Meanwhile, the other kids check out the candy wall! There are so many snacks to choose from!

Now that they know the rules, the kids go for a ride.

The kids take the zipline
down to the jungle.
It's super fast—and super fun!

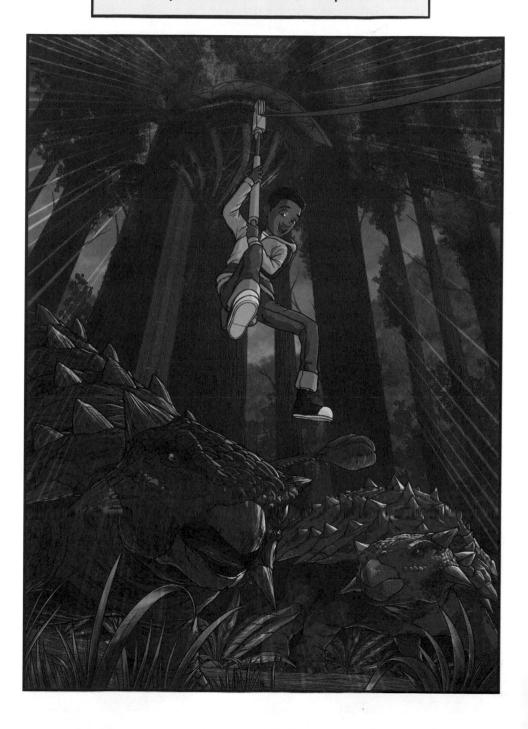

That night, Kenji and Darius sneak out while the others sleep. Darius wants to see more dinosaurs. Brooklynn records it all for her channel.

Where are you going?

Unfortunately, they accidentally wander into the Raptor area!

Brooklynn presses a button
to help them escape.
There's just one problem—

Wrong button,
Brooklynn!

RUN!

Darius looks around
for something
to help them get out.
Roxie and Dave arrive
to help!
They throw meat
into the Raptors' pen.

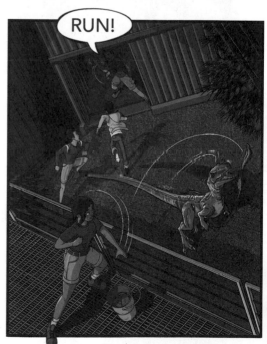

The counselors are glad the kids are safe.
But they're also mad!
They caught the boys breaking the rules.

You guys are in big trouble!

And I know just the punishment!

23

Darius and Kenji will miss
the trip to the genetics lab.
That's where dinosaurs are made!
The other kids go inside.

The scientists are very busy.
Making dinosaurs isn't easy!

The genetics lab is cool.
But some parts are top-secret.

Time for you to leave.

Kenji never learns.
While the others are at the lab,
he sneaks Darius into the tunnels
that run under the park.
But it's a bad idea to leave
the tunnels.
Because if you do . . .

It's been a really long day.
The tired kids meet back at camp.

Darius drifts off to sleep
dreaming of dinosaurs.
But the best part is . . .

. . . Darius doesn't have to just dream about them anymore! The adventure is just beginning!

Woo-hoo!!